By Gail Herman

Illustrated by Duendes del Sur

SCHOLASTIC INC.

New York   Toronto   London   Auckland   Sydney
Mexico City   New Delhi   Hong Kong   Buenos Aires

ISBN 0-439-34116-7

18                         08                         13/0

Designed by Maria Stasavage
Printed in the U.S.A.
First Scholastic printing, November 2002

The gang was riding around the parking lot at Coolsville High School. It was the day of the big football game. The parking lot was packed.

Fred, Velma, and Daphne looked for a parking space.

*Zzzzz.*

In the back seat, Shaggy and Scooby snored.

"There are no parking spaces!" Fred said.

Velma nodded. "Fans have been here for hours!" she said.

"Go! Go!" A roar swept over the van.

"And everyone's been shouting for hours," Daphne added.

Just then a loud buzzer sounded.
"The game is starting!" said Fred.
Shaggy and Scooby were suddenly wide-awake.

"We have to hurry!" Shaggy cried. He and
Scooby raced out of the van. "We have to
get to the snack stand!"

A few minutes later, Shaggy and Scooby
stood in line.

"What do you say, good buddy," Shaggy
said. "Hot dogs with the works?"

"Rulp!" Scooby gulped.

"Yeah, I'm hungry, too," Shaggy agreed.

Scooby shook his head. He pointed to the front of the line.

"Gulp!" Shaggy stared.

A strange-looking creature stared back. Then it disappeared.

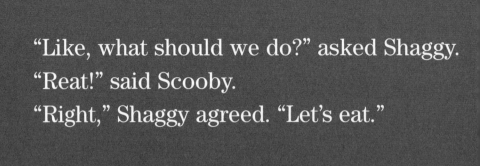

"Like, what should we do?" asked Shaggy.

"Reat!" said Scooby.

"Right," Shaggy agreed. "Let's eat."

Chomp! Chomp! Shaggy and Scooby tried to eat and carry their food at the same time.

"Hey! Let's get a Coolsville High backpack!" said Shaggy. "We can stash the grub in there!"

"Rrrrr, rrrrr, grrrrr." Strange voices filled the air.

Two more creatures stepped close to Shaggy and Scooby.

They were orange. Striped. And muttering in a crazy language.

"They're shaped like people," Shaggy whispered. "But they can't be people."

"Raliens!" cried Scooby.

"Aliens!" cried Shaggy.

They dropped their food and ran.

They didn't get far. "Ruh-uh!" said Scooby. He pointed to the sky.

"Zoinks!" Shaggy gasped, staring at the sky.

High above them hovered a spaceship. An alien spaceship!

"Quick!" Shaggy pointed across the field. "Let's find the gang."

The buddies stumbled through the stands. All at once, Scooby stopped. "Rore raliens!"

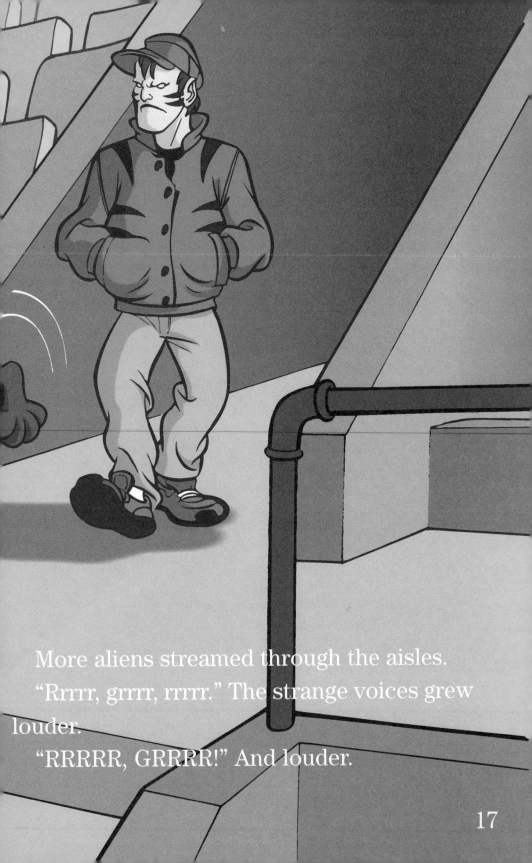

More aliens streamed through the aisles.

"Rrrrr, grrrr, rrrrr." The strange voices grew louder.

"RRRRR, GRRRR!" And louder.

"The aliens are taking over!" Shaggy cried. He and Scooby leaped onto the football field. "Everyone! Follow us!"

Plop! A football dropped into Shaggy's hands. He looked to his right. More aliens were coming. Bigger, stronger ones. He looked to his left. Still more aliens!

Shaggy took off, straight down the center of the field.

Scooby's legs spun like wheels as he tried to keep up.

Crash! Boom! Aliens fell like bowling pins.

The buddies raced to the end of the field.
They dove under the goalpost.
"Rouchdown!" shouted Scooby.

A crowd of aliens swooped down. Shaggy shook them off. "Like, what do you want?" he cried.

"RRRRR! GRRRR! RRRRR!"

Shaggy didn't know what to do. So he tossed the football.

"Rrrrr! Grrrr!" One alien scooped it up. Then, in a flash, all the aliens raced away.

Shaggy and Scooby found the rest of the gang.

"It's weird, man," Shaggy told the others. "All the aliens wanted was a football. And now they're going back to their spaceship."

"Aliens?" Velma repeated. "Spaceship?" She looked up at the sky. "That's a blimp," she told Shaggy and Scooby. "The kind you see at football games."

"Call it what you want, Velma," Shaggy told her. "But all these orange-and-black space-men need to get home somehow!"

"Those aren't aliens." Velma shook her head. "Those are fans wearing face paint. Orange and black to look like tigers. For the Terrytown Tigers football team. And some are football players in uniform."

"But what about the strange noises? Rrrrr? Grrrr?" Shaggy asked.

"That's the Tigers' cheer!" said Fred.

"Their voices sound funny from shouting so much!" Daphne added.

Shaggy's face fell. "And to think!" he
moaned. "We dropped all that food when we
ran away!"

Just then the Coolsville coach walked over.

"Good job carrying the ball, boys," the coach told Scooby and Shaggy. "You really had those Tigers going. Do you want Coolsville jackets? Caps? A team football?"

Scooby and Shaggy shook their heads.
"How about a team dinner?" said Shaggy.
"Scooby-Dooby-Doo!" barked Scooby